BRAINSTORM!

WRITTEN BY

ILLUSTRATED BY

REBECCA GARDYN LEVINGTON

KATE KRONREIF

To Ari and Milo,
Wishing you a huge downpour
of ideas! :)

PUBLISHED BY SLEEPING BEAR PRESS

Teacher says it's time to write. UGH. I clench my pencil tight.

I peek outside—
it's gloomy, gray.

Cloudy.

Like my brain today.

I think

and think . . .

but nothing's there.

I slump.

I sulk.

I sigh.

I stare.

But then . . .

KER-PLINK!

I feel a drop.

One tiny thought.

Then more...

PLIP!

PLOP!

Words and pictures . . .

Pitter!
Pat!

drip, then drizzle.

Plunk!

Plonk!

SPLAT!

LEAPING LIZARDS

An easy breeze . . .
becomes a blast
of funny phrases flying past.

SHEEP SHOULD SHOWER IN A SHED

BYE BYE BUTTERFLY

SALTY STRAWBERRY SALSA

PRICKLY PINE CONES

Whoa! I laugh, as nouns swirl 'round.

An adverb knocks me to the ground!

JOKINGLY

Gusts of adjectives blow by.

Verb clouds swell and multiply.

SHOUT

CREATE

SNEEZE

WHISTLE

ENERGETIC

FANTASTIC

WET SILLY

FUZZY

WHOOSH!

A happy memory
gushes, rushes over me.

TEDDY BEAR UNDERCOVER

THE DOLPHIN WHO COULDN'T TANGO

HIPPOS WHO HOP

THANKSGIVING ON THE MOON

Topics toss my clothes and hair!

Titles twirl me everywhere!

Questions spill down
from the sky—
HOW?
and WHEN?
and WHERE?
and WHY?

POW!

A sharp and sudden FLASH!

BOOM!

A grumble-rumble . . .

CRASH!

Huge ideas flowing fast!

I smile and spread my arms.

"AT LAST!"

I dance in puddles.

SPLISH! SPLASH! STOMP!

My boots get mucky.

SQUASH!

SPLOSH!

WHOMP!

THE CLOWN LEFT THE CIRCUS TO BECOME A DOCTOR

ONCE UPON A TIME. TWO DUCKS AND A PONY BECAME FRIENDS

PICKLED PEPPERS

I pounce and play, embrace the storm,
as sentences begin to form.

SHE COULDN'T WAIT FOR HER FIRST TRIP TO VENUS

BUT SUDDENLY SHE HAD AN IDEA

IT WAS SUPPOSED TO

SHE HAD NEVER TO

SUDDENLY

SHE NEVER SUPPOSED TO THIS

END WAS

SO THE ROBOT FLEW TO MEXICO

Beginnings, middles, endings fall. I try my best to catch them all!

I'm sopping wet with wacky thoughts
of characters and twisty plots,

of images and bits of dreams,
of settings, scenes, and quirky themes!

I tip my head and drink them in,
as stories soak my clothes and skin.

And then . . .

it stops.

It's over.

Done.

The clouds float off

and out comes . . .

sun.

I look around and only see . . . a flood of possibility.

A rainbow fills the sky with light.

My mind is clear.

So now . . .

I WRITE.

CLOUDY WITH A CHANCE OF IDEAS!
Inspire a downpour of creativity with these writing prompts:

You have magically turned into your favorite animal! What are you? What do you do for fun?

Think of a special toy or object and tell the story of when and how you got it.

Be a salesman! How would you sell me a: broken umbrella, pen out of ink, cat with no hair, etc.

If kids ruled the world . . .

Pick a word. Set a timer and write about it for one minute. No stopping!

Watch a movie with the sound off. What do you think the characters are saying? Write a script.

You have been granted three wishes! What are they? How will you use them? How do you think your wishes will make things better/worse?

You have been granted one superpower— what is it? How will you use it?

Create a new holiday. What would you celebrate and how?

Pick a color. What does it look, feel, taste, smell, and sound like?

Your favorite board or video game just came to life and you jumped into the action! What happens next?

Look out the window— what's the first thing you see? Describe it in as much detail as you can.

Describe the first time you ever tried . . .

You get the chance to meet your favorite hero! What do you say? What do they say?

Find a picture of yourself as a baby. What do you think you were doing and feeling at that moment?

Look at a photograph. What do you imagine happened right before or after the picture was taken?

What does home feel like?

In what other ways could this be used? (common objects: fork, rubber band, paper clip, banana, lost sock, etc., or uncommon objects: a plastic glove filled with air, an unusual kitchen tool, etc.)

A TORNADO OF TERMINOLOGY

Adjective: A word that describes a person, place, thing, or idea (noun or pronoun), such as "big," "red," "funny," "dirty," and "small." Example: The **red** dress was made of cotton.

Adverb: A word that describes an action (verb) or adjective and answers the question When? Where? How? How much? How long? or How often? Most adverbs are formed by adding "-ly" to an adjective, as in "happily," "gently," "quietly," and "slowly." Example: The sloth walks **slowly**. "Slowly" answers the question "How does the sloth walk?"

Characters: The people (animals, monsters, etc.) that participate in the action of your story.

Noun: A word that refers to a person, place, thing, or idea, such as "teacher," "bedroom," "book," "dog," and "ice cream shop." Example: The **spider** spins a **web**. A proper noun is a type of noun that refers to a specific person, place, or thing and is almost always capitalized, such as "Abraham Lincoln," "San Francisco," and "the White House."

Phrase: Two or more words that go together but do not form a full sentence. Examples: "super smelly cheese" and "wacky weather."

Plot: The order of events in your story—what happens in the beginning, middle, and end. Also called a "story line" or "narrative."

Pronoun: A word that is used instead of a noun or proper noun, such as "I," "he," "she," "they," "we," and "it." Example: **He** likes to play in puddles!

Scene: A part of your story in which one specific event occurs.

Setting: The time and location in which your story takes place.

Theme: The big idea behind your story. Example: If your story is about a kid who has to practice a lot to get on the gymnastics team, your theme might be: "kids who work hard can achieve their goals."

Topic: The overall subject of your story. Topics can be big or small. For example, "sports," "nature," and "health" are big topics. Within these big topics are smaller topics like "baseball," "birds," and "getting sick." And within those topics are even smaller topics like "the Yankees," "hummingbirds," and "sneezes."

Verb: Words that describe or show action, such as "sing," "dance," "run," and "clap." Example: The little boy **dances** all the time.

For Sam and Daniel. May you never tire of playing in puddles of possibility. And for Joel. Your endless downpour of encouragement means everything.

—R.G.L.

For sweet Silas

—K.K.

Text Copyright © 2022 Rebecca Gardyn Levington
Illustration Copyright © 2022 Kate Kronreif
Design Copyright © 2022 Sleeping Bear Press

Sleeping Bear Press™

2395 South Huron Parkway, Suite 200
Ann Arbor, MI 48104
www.sleepingbearpress.com

Printed and bound in the United States.

10 9 8 7 6 5 4 3 2 1

Library of Congress Cataloging-in-Publication Data

Names: Levington, Rebecca Gardyn, author. | Kronreif, Kate, illustrator.
Title: Brainstorm! / by Rebecca Gardyn Levington ; illustrated by Kate Kronreif.
Description: Ann Arbor, MI : Sleeping Bear Press, [2022] | Audience: Ages 6-10. |
Summary: A child, struggling with what to write about, is swept up in a whirlwind of words, pictures, and ideas, until she finds herself caught in a downpour of her own creativity. Includes writing prompts and glossary.
Identifiers: LCCN 2022006573 | ISBN 9781534111486 (hardcover)
Subjects: CYAC: Stories in rhyme. | Authorship—Fiction. | Creative ability—Fiction. | Storms—Fiction. | LCGFT: Picture books. | Stories in rhyme.
Classification: LCC PZ8.3.L5776 Br 2022 | DDC [E]—dc23
LC record available at https://lccn.loc.gov/2022006573